Copyright © 1999 by Nord-Süd Verlag AG, Gossau Zürich, Switzerland
First published in Switzerland under the title *Rodolfo kommt*
English translation copyright © 1999 by North-South Books Inc.
All rights reserved. No part of this book may be reproduced or utilized in any form or by any means, electronic or
mechanical, including photocopying, recording, or any information storage and retrieval system, without permission in
writing from the publisher.

First published in the United States, Great Britain, Canada, Australia, and New Zealand in 1999 by North-South Books,
an imprint of Nord-Süd Verlag AG, Gossau Zürich, Switzerland. Distributed in the United States by North-South Books Inc.,
New York.

Library of Congress Cataloging-in-Publication Data is available.
A CIP catalogue record for this book is available from The British Library.

ISBN 0-7358-1067-2 (trade binding) 10 9 8 7 6 5 4 3 2 1
ISBN 0-7358-1068-0 (library binding) 10 9 8 7 6 5 4 3 2 1
Printed in Belgium

For more information about our books, and the authors and artists
who create them, visit our web site: http://www.northsouth.com

HIDING HORATIO

By Udo Weigelt

Illustrated by
Alexander Reichstein

Translated by
J. Alison James

North-South Books
New York / London

The animals in the forest chattered with excitement. Something was approaching from the river, an immense animal unlike anything they had ever seen before. Slowly but steadily it tramped towards them.

"What do we do? What do we do?" squeaked Mouse anxiously. "What if it wants to eat us?"

"We have to defend ourselves!" cried Badger and all agreed, particularly Squirrel.

But Fox said softly: "I think we ought to wait and watch. Perhaps the animal is friendly, or maybe it will pass by without stopping."

The animals thought this over and quickly agreed that Fox was right. So they hid, waiting to see what the strange animal would do.

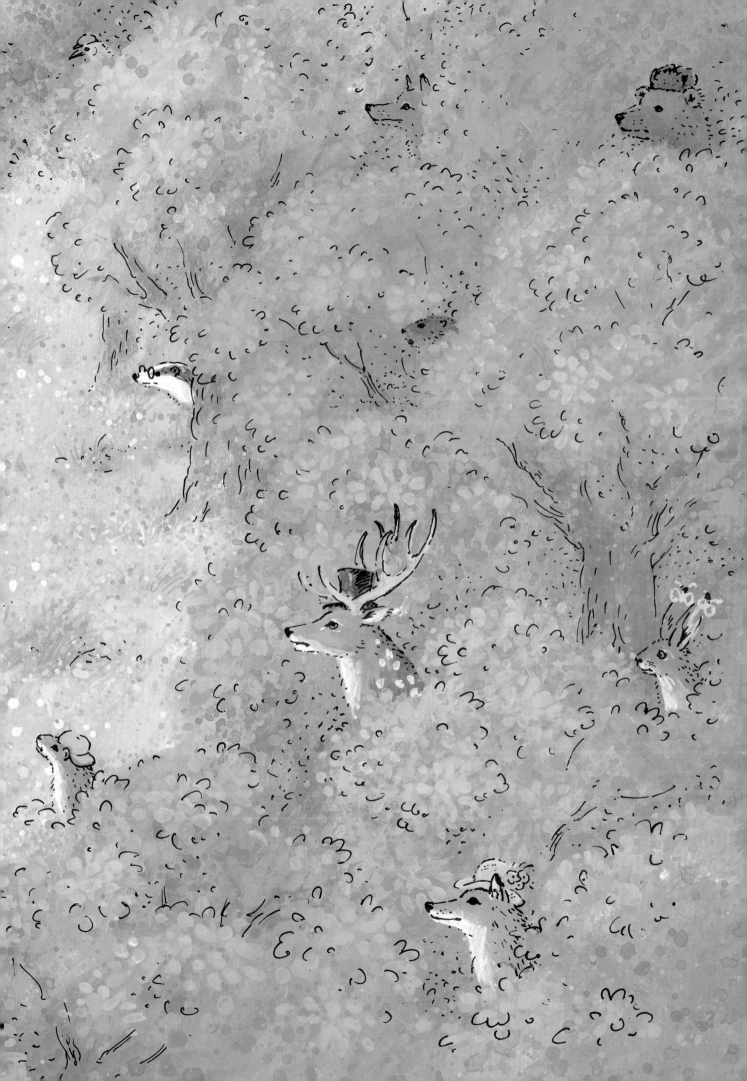

From their hiding places, the animals watched intently as the creature lumbered through the woods. Squirrel had nuts ready to throw, in case of emergency. But as she looked more closely, she saw that it didn't actually look so terribly dangerous. It was just huge. The other animals saw this too. But because the creature was so very big, everyone decided to stay hidden.

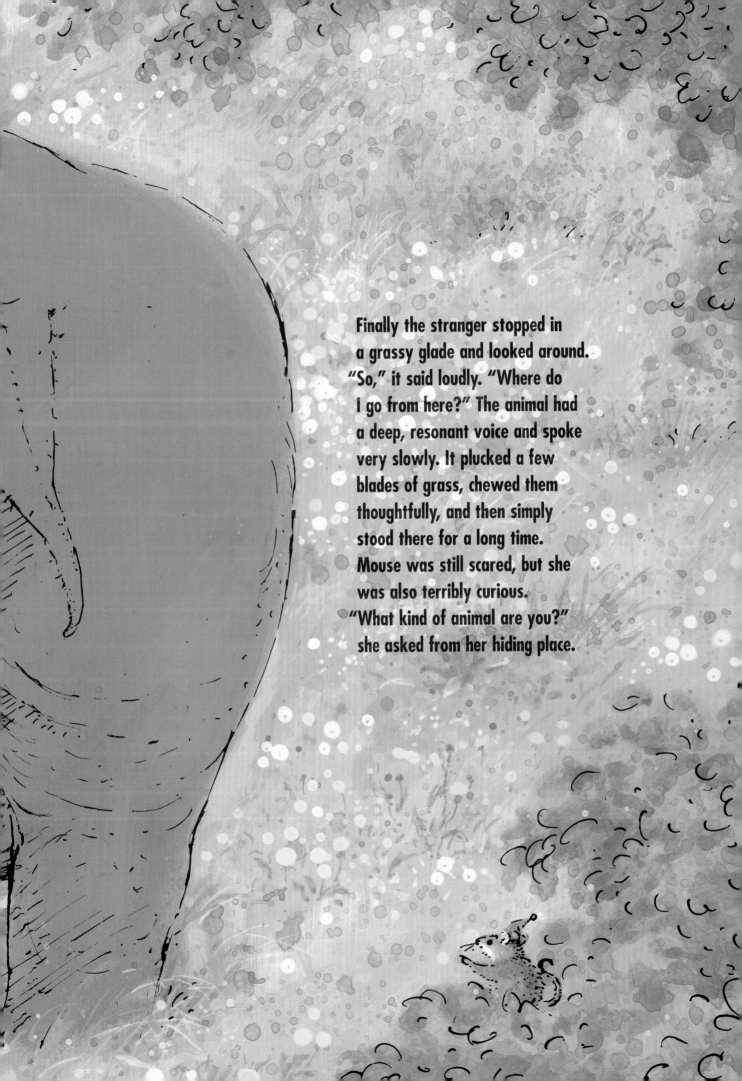

Finally the stranger stopped in
a grassy glade and looked around.
"So," it said loudly. "Where do
I go from here?" The animal had
a deep, resonant voice and spoke
very slowly. It plucked a few
blades of grass, chewed them
thoughtfully, and then simply
stood there for a long time.
Mouse was still scared, but she
was also terribly curious.
"What kind of animal are you?"
she asked from her hiding place.

"Hello? Is someone there?" asked the strange animal.

"It's me!" peeped Mouse. "But what kind of animal are you?"

"I . . . am . . . a . . . hippopotamus," said the animal, turning to where the voice had come from. "And you?"

"A mouse." Quickly she nipped across the grass to another bush where she had a better view.

"Aah, now I see you," said the hippopotamus. "Are you alone, or are there other animals in this vicinity?"

All the animals answered at once: "Yes! I'm here! I'm Deer."

"And I'm Badger!"

"And I'm Wild Boar!"

All the animals introduced themselves and cautiously poked their heads out of their hiding places.

The hippopotamus bowed. "My name is Horatio. I am a hippopotamus on the run."

Horatio seemed to be truly friendly. In any case, he was quite polite, and because of that, even the shyest animals now came out.

But all of a sudden his immense mouth opened wide, showing all his teeth, and . . .

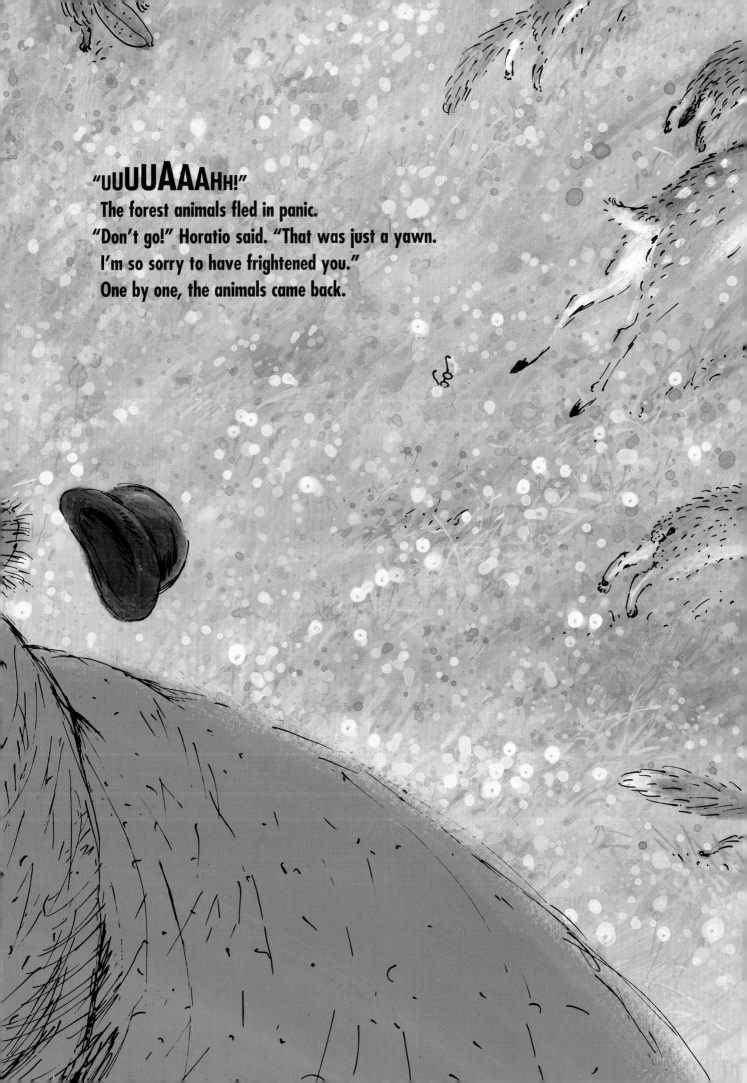

"uuUUAAAHH!"
The forest animals fled in panic.
"Don't go!" Horatio said. "That was just a yawn.
I'm so sorry to have frightened you."
One by one, the animals came back.

"I yawned," said Horatio, "because I am so very tired. I have been walking a long way."
"Where did you come from?" asked Mouse curiously.
Horatio explained that he'd been on display with a small circus. But the new owners didn't want a hippopotamus. They were going to sell him, so he ran away.
"Actually," Horatio said, "I thought I would go home, to Africa. But after today, I believe it might be too great a distance for me to walk. Therefore . . . I wonder . . ." Horatio shifted his weight in embarrassment.
"This is such a beautiful spot . . . I wonder if you would mind if I stayed here. At least for a while . . . oh excuse me," he said suddenly and "UUUUAAAHHH!" his mouth stretched open again in a yawn.
But this time the animals did not run away.

"Well, I think we ought to let Horatio stay with us," said Mouse. "He can't go back to the circus and Africa is much too far away."

The other animals thought it over. A hippopotamus in the woods was certainly unusual, but maybe that was a good thing, and besides, where else was he to go? Everyone agreed Horatio should stay.

And just in time. Right then Rabbit raced up.

"Watch out! Watch out! Men are coming. Watch out! Two dangerous men!"

"Oh dear," said Horatio. "I believe they're searching for me. I'm not hard to spot. They will certainly catch me!"

"We have to stop them!" Mouse cried. "Who's got an idea?"

Weasel smiled slyly. "I have," she said.

And then everything happened quickly—surprisingly quickly for a slow-moving hippopotamus.

The men were hunters who were indeed searching
for Horatio. They tracked him to the shore of the lake.
But then the tracks suddenly stopped.
"That's impossible," one of the hunters said.
"How could a huge hippo vanish into thin air?"
He leaned against a boulder.
"I don't have a clue," said the other, shaking his head.
"But the tracks stop here. So let's look somewhere else."

That they did—until it occurred to one hunter that he'd never seen that large boulder beside the lake before. They raced back. But the boulder was gone.

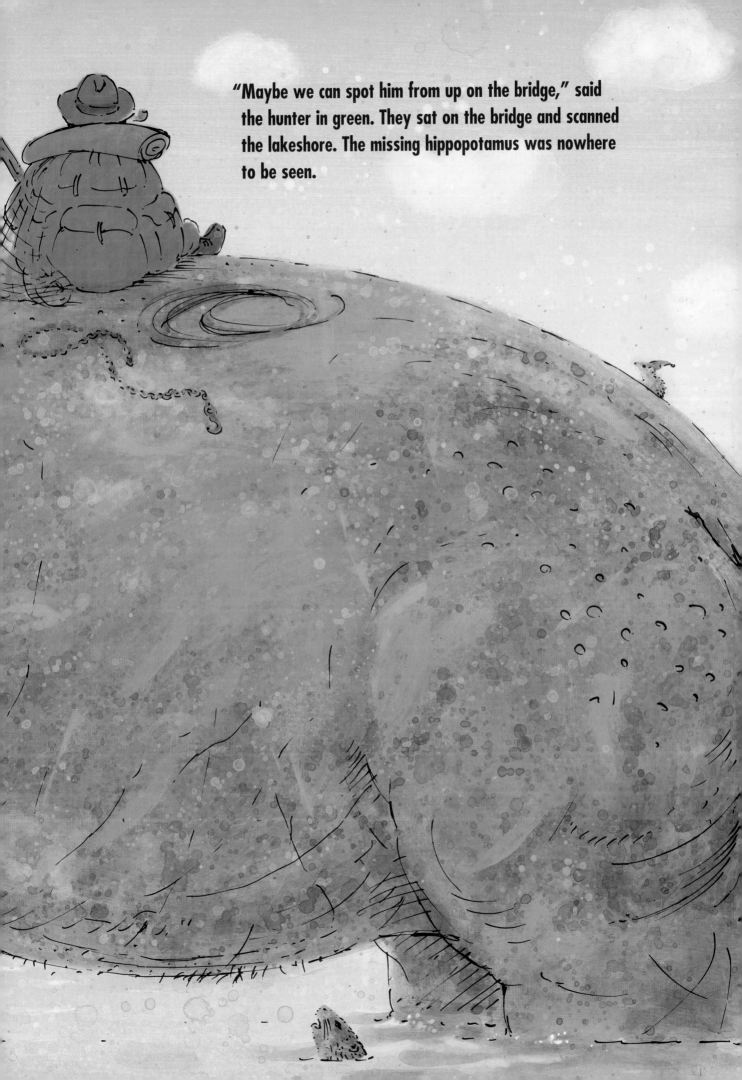

"Maybe we can spot him from up on the bridge," said the hunter in green. They sat on the bridge and scanned the lakeshore. The missing hippopotamus was nowhere to be seen.

The two men were getting annoyed.
They climbed up on tree stumps to get
a better look.

"Hey, when was that bridge built?" one hunter asked the other. "I don't remember a bridge." But when they went back to the shore for a second look, the bridge was gone.

Horatio had found a new hiding place with some help
from Beaver. The men searched for hours, but finally
gave up. As soon as they were gone, Horatio rose from
his hiding place and found a spot in the sun to dry.
All the animals surrounded him.
"You have saved my life," he said. "I would like to
thank you with a concert. I enjoy singing tremendously.
If you are so inclined, return to this place at moonrise."

Of course all the animals came. Having a hippopotamus in their woods was already extraordinary. But one who could sing!
It was a wonderful evening. All the animals spruced themselves up and put on their finery. Rustling excitedly, they waited for the moon to rise. A great hush fell over them as Horatio began to sing. His voice was deep and passionate, rhythmic and rolling. As the curtain of stars fell over the final song, their applause was so resounding that Horatio knew he had found a new home.